Samuel French Acting Edition

I0591989

Jack Was Kind

by Tracy Thorne

FOR PRODUCTION INQUIRIES

UNITED STATES AND CANADA
info@concordtheatricals.com
1-866-979-0447

UNITED KINGDOM AND EUROPE
licensing@concordtheatricals.co.uk
020-7054-7200

Each title is subject to availability from Concord Theatricals Corp., depending upon country of performance. Please be aware that *JACK WAS KIND* may not be licensed by Concord Theatricals Corp. in your territory. Professional and amateur producers should contact the nearest Concord Theatricals Corp. office or licensing partner to verify availability.

No one shall make any changes in this title(s) for the purpose of production. No part of this book may be reproduced, stored in a retrieval system, scanned, uploaded, or transmitted in any form, by any means, now known or yet to be invented, including mechanical, electronic, digital, photocopying, recording, videotaping, or otherwise, without the prior written permission of the publisher. No one shall share this title(s), or any part of this title(s), through any social media or file hosting websites.

For all inquiries regarding motion picture, television, online/digital and other media rights, please contact Concord Theatricals Corp.

MUSIC AND THIRD-PARTY MATERIALS USE NOTE

Licensees are solely responsible for obtaining formal written permission from copyright owners to use copyrighted music and/or other copyrighted third-party materials (e.g., artworks, logos) in the performance of this play and are strongly cautioned to do so. If no such permission is obtained by the licensee, then the licensee must use only original music and materials that the licensee owns and controls. Licensees are solely responsible and liable for clearances of all third-party copyrighted materials, including without limitation music, and shall indemnify the copyright owners of the play(s) and their licensing agent, Concord Theatricals Corp., against any costs, expenses, losses and liabilities arising from the use of such copyrighted third-party materials by licensees. For music, please contact the appropriate music licensing authority in your territory for the rights to any incidental music.

IMPORTANT BILLING AND CREDIT REQUIREMENTS

If you have obtained performance rights to this title, please refer to your licensing agreement for important billing and credit requirements.

JACK WAS KIND premiered online, in a virtual production, on September 10, 2020. It was produced by All For One Theater (Michael Wolk, Artistic Director; Nicholas Cotz, Executive & Producing Director) in association with Consulting Producer, Jami Floyd. The production was directed by Nicholas Cotz. The cast was as follows:

MARY. . . . . .Tracy Thorne

CHARACTERS

MARY – A woman. Any race. Late forties/early fifties. Middle-class and wearing her Sunday best. Mary is modest and unaccustomed to being the center of attention...not a natural raconteur. That said, she works hard to get her facts straight and is unafraid to do so. In other words, Mary is brave and serious. She's been driven to it.

TIME

Now

SETTING

Mary's home...it's straight-down-the-middle lovely.
She is alone.

AUTHOR'S NOTES

1. In spite of her initial reticence, and because she is alone, Mary's talk flows. She does not judge herself as she goes, sometimes finds what she says funny, and only stops speaking when the text says "wait." Her waits can be very long, or very short, but Mary *always* waits where indicated. Give it a try, it works.

2. When dialogue is in quotation marks and italics, it belongs to Mary's daughter, and Mary speaks in her daughter's voice.

This play is for my dazzling daughters, Bella and Mabel.

It's the accumulation of insignificant things like this that has made me the person I am.
– Haruki Murakami

*(**MARY** tells us a story while filming herself on her computer – perhaps we even see her on another screen. To start, a Post-It covers the computer's camera. **MARY** pulls the Post-It away and gazes awkwardly at the camera's green light before abruptly looking for the record button.)*

MARY. Did I press record – yes.

(She looks nervously into the camera.)

I...ummm...wanted to say that...I read this in a magazine. A Japanese man wrote it. His name is...

(She looks down at a page torn from a magazine.)

...Haruki Murakami, if I'm pronouncing that right.

(Reads.) "It's the accumulation of insignificant things like this that has made me the person I am."

(Wait.)

Okay.

(Wait.)

How could I just sit there? For ten years that's the question? Over and over, from people I've never met, that's the 64,000-dollar question, how could I just sit there? "I don't know," is the answer. Only now, my nineteen-year-old daughter tells me, *"That's a bad answer, Mom, it's unacceptable."* She's a nineteen-year-old expert, right? And I don't like that she condescends to me, but she doesn't care and flat out asks me herself, *"How could you just sit there, Mom?"* She's never asked before, I always hoped she wouldn't, ridiculous of me because the day was bound to come. And she just keeps going, she's home from college for the summer, full of beans, saying, *"Finally, I've taken a class worth the tuition. Constitutional Law, Mom, what do you think of that?"* I think she's trying to threaten me, that's what I think of that and it works, I feel threatened, but also, her brain's exploded, it's like a water main break, and a water main break's not good but the spectacle of the gush is breathtaking. I'm scared to death of my daughter now but my eyes are glued to her all the same. I keep wondering if she'll go into the law, like her father, like Jack – not like me, hardly, I'm the administrator for our little suburb, you know, order the Do Not Litter signs, things like that, it's a paid position but, things like that. And anyway, people say I never talk, Jack does all the talking. Except since my daughter came home I talk more, for years groups have asked me but I always said no, of course I said no...but recently I accepted a couple of invitations...I talked...told stories...then I thought of recording some stories, so I can do what I want with them, send them wherever, I guess if you're watching I sent them somewhere...maybe *because* I feel threatened. And I don't blame my daughter for anything.

(*Wait.*)

Some people want me to stop...telling stories...to cease and desist, I don't think those people will like this very much.

(*Wait.*)

My kids love videos.

(*Wait.*)

Nearly two years of a nonsensically overpriced education results in our daughter having no observable intellectual curiosity, then boom, the match ignites, when it's personal it ignites, and now she wants to know, but I don't want her to know, *I* don't know, though sometimes I wonder if I *do*, that's a thing, right? *"Really Mom, you don't know how you could just sit there?"* That's what she says to me. So I guess this is how it starts for my daughter, maybe for me too, funny it starts at the end. But then I don't know if it's the end, or *do* I know if it's the end, I don't know what I know and now I'm threatening myself. *"Don't you think you should know, Mom, frankly I'm appalled you don't."* She says that, too.

(Wait.)

Appalled?

(Wait.)

Well, why *not* talk then, tell a story, maybe two, and anyway, "Tell Me A Story" are the four greatest words in the English language so, shall I tell you a story...about Jack? And even if you don't like the idea, might be hard to resist, right? Now, for anyone who's never heard of Jack...well...*is* there anyone who's never heard of Jack? And I wonder, maybe, if it's possible, I don't know, but I wonder...if there *is* an answer to the 64,000-dollar question, for my daughter, she'd like an answer, how *could* I just sit there? I'd like to give her an answer. It's the least I can do.

(Wait.)

Okay, in case you think you know everything about my husband Jack, here's one thing you don't know. He takes singing lessons. Has for twenty years. And amazingly...he's still not good. Another thing you don't know, once a year, he hires a piano player to come to the house so he can sing me love songs – I bet you *do* know he's not a coward. Even though Jack sounds kind of bad, I like it very much, I can't do things like that, oh no, but I love things like that, and Jack loves that I love it...get the picture?

(Wait.)

What else about Jack? Altar boy. Exceptional student. Loving son. Family man. Devout Catholic and proud steward of our church, Sacred Hearts of Jesus and Mary. And of course his distinguished career in the law that could not be any more consequential, mustn't forget that. But. The most important thing...Jack is kind. Most important. His face always composed, looking like it is his privilege to listen. Jack draws power by making his face look like he is privileged to listen, by specifically putting his face in position...I know, right? He deploys this look far and wide, is famous for it, but his trick – Jack's very good trick – is customizing the look. As in, he'll give a whiff of something distinctive, a hint of special, so every person feels *her* 'Jack' look, *his* 'Jack' look, is the most searching, probing, piercing 'Jack' look – mine, however, *is* the most searching, probing, piercing...see?

(Wait.)

Okay, *my* 'Jack' look? Its mission is to make me feel 'hanging-on-my-every-word' interesting, a sore point from my beat-up childhood, you bet, and Jack knows it. Not literally beat-up, but more like...dented...from childhood in a void, that much 'nothing' can really crash the car. So *my* 'Jack' look makes me feel 'happy-like-I've-never-felt-happy' happy, which he also knows, and making me happy makes him happy, it's the thing that does the most and, very important, that last part is a secret...shhhhhh, Jack always says, "Don't tell anyone." *Why* is it a secret? Well...I never ask. *Why* don't I ever ask? Well...maybe I don't want to know. But Jack *needs* to make me happy, his face goes shiny when he does, I have no idea why, but making me happy is everything for Jack. I am everything for Jack. And that sounds like a dream, doesn't it? But maybe I should say, being everything to another person is deceptively not wonderful all the time. And why am I everything? *Am I everything?*

(Wait.)

Of course the children make him very happy, that Eli and Flo are everything is also true, or so the story goes. He'll do anything they ask, that's a fact. Even if he's having a hard day, even if plaintiffs are clamoring, or defendants, lives may hang in the balance but Jack gets such a kick out of being their big shot. Once there was a huge case about to derail and everyone was working twenty-hour days. But Jack had given Eli tickets to the World Series for his birthday and no way was Jack going to miss it – disappoint his boy? – that's not Jack, so he called in sick. Only someone's husband thought he saw Jack at the game, which got around, and Jack's boss called the house – the big boss. I worried something like this might happen but since Jack says he does twice the work in half the time he believed the right choice was to come through for his son and, furthermore, he said he didn't need to suffer with the herd. I'd decided not to answer the phone while they were at the game, just in case, but when it rang, I don't know why, the ringing made me angry, I got a hard feeling in my stomach, and I picked up the phone. The big boss asked to speak to Jack, he didn't ask nicely, but he didn't frighten me, and with no plan to do it – and not nicely myself – I said Jack had a fever of 104 and if he wanted Jack to come in the next day he had to let Jack sleep, all while making it clear I thought his calling was inappropriate. I stopped the big boss in his tracks, by lying and being nasty. And then the anger drained off and I felt queasy instead, why did I lie? Eli would have been fine going to the game with me, especially since I thought Jack should have gone to work, the herd should have been his priority, but I lied like that anyway and I don't know why I was nasty, I guess I was put into a position where I had to be nasty.

(Wait.)

I'm not nasty. That's not me. But never resist a generous impulse, Jack was doing it for his boy, right? Like I said, Jack is kind. *And* he's something else too – before she said anything ten years ago, before I ever heard of her, he was something else too – but what? It's never clear and everything she said makes it less clear. Yes, I have thoughts, and my thoughts can make me...sad, which then gets me afraid, but of what, afraid of what... Jack? Eli and Flo are not, I don't think so, but does a little bit of uncertainty make me afraid of Jack? And does not knowing make me more afraid? Or do I know more than I think? I don't know what I know, I said that before, see the problem?

(Wait.)

"Mom, you do understand, **you're** *the problem."* No, I don't understand. So how can I answer the 64,000-dollar question?

(Wait.)

Let's go back to Jack's face, I always do, to his dazzling listening face, to the considerable power he still draws – *I know* – from everyone who can't get enough of his dazzling listening face. Flo used to say, *"It's like an invitation, Mommy."* And sure, it's a little different since...now...but *before* I bet it never crossed anyone's mind to suspect Jack's face. That takes time, exposure, to get past being drawn in and dazzled by Jack's dazzling face. But sometimes I see a different face. I know the first time I saw it, he was watching the game – oh, Jack's sports mad, always, no time anymore, but on weekends if he can, football, basketball, whatever, captain of all his high school teams, he's that guy. Okay, it was halftime and the commercials were blaring – you know how sometimes the ads are louder than the show? – and I saw the face, the different one. It's kind of a mad face, and there's a sound that goes with it, a 'trying not to groan' sound.

(She makes the sound. It's weird.)

Hard to tell what that means, right? And it made me sad, which made me afraid...so I asked him about it, and he said, "The game was so good, I felt excited and had to let it out." But I thought, 'The game wasn't on, it was a truck commercial. No, you were mad, toxic and mad, and you tried to stuff it back down your throat, that sound was you trying, I'd bet on it.' I didn't say that but I thought it. And I'm never sure what that face means. Funny the things between married people that don't ever get cleared up, huh?

(Wait.)

But wait, you know the face...on the day...that was the face.

(Wait.)

I will admit to wondering, and *before* I even wondered, if other people – we know some do now, but *before* – if other people ever felt...ruffled by Jack, his listening face, it's just always so much. How about at work, what happens if you feel ruffled by the look on a person's face? Even if that person is kind, the *kindest*? On a personal level, well, maybe there's chemistry, but at work could you ever feel...played? By a look? I can imagine it, and *not* just at work, in other situations, I can. And all the looks must be hard work, *remembering to make them*?! Is the power we give him – I imagine an electric current keeping him all lit up – worth the work? And pulling a face can make you powerful? Do we surrender our power to Jack – and he has a lot of power, doesn't he? – because he pulls a face, makes us feel fascinating by pulling a face, are we idiots or what?

Then again, maybe Jack knows, the *feeling* of kindness is as good as it gets. People are overcome by the *feeling* of Jack's kindness, I was overcome the *most*, spellbound and hypnotized, right now even, others too, still.

(Wait.)

But who really knows if he *is* kind, right? I wonder if he really knows, *what* he really knows. That's what I wonder when I'm not devastated that boom, there went my life.

(Wait.)

Full disclosure, I am not going to tell you Jack beat me up, emotionally abused me, he did not. I am not going to tell you our children suffered a grim fate at Jack's brute hand, they did not. I *am* going to tell you Jack loved us. I am going to tell you, for twenty-six years, Jack healed my oldest wounds, Jack made me his sweetheart, Jack made me interesting. That's what Jack did.

(Wait.)

But I don't know what else Jack did.

(Wait.)

"Mom, to be perfectly blunt, I'm finding it hard to believe you." No, it's true. But I'm trying. Now I am.

(Wait.)

Wait, here's a story...this one's about my father, he's the old wound part, then fathers often are, right? But if we're talking about Jack, maybe my father is important – I bet they'd both find that surprising, when it occurred to me two seconds ago *I* did. Okay, in a hundred years, no one would ever say Jack and my father are alike, my father is not kind, my father does not listen – far as I know he never listened and seems impossible he ever was kind. My father's face isn't composed either, 'composed face' people are billed as still-waters-run-deep types, but that's not my father, he's not deep. And he's not quiet, he's loud and scratchy, like stripping-paint-with-a-sharp-tool scratchy. Whatever, my father's opinions don't accommodate other opinions, which never feels kind and always gets loud. And if ever there were a better opinion out there, my father didn't listen to it so he'd never know. Now, should I wonder why? Is he a tragic figure – yet still towering, of course – because he has a character defect for which I should feel compassion? Or do I need to duck and cover because a monster wants to rip my skin off and eat me alive? Tricky one, don't you think?

(Wait.)

Boy, when a daughter's got nothing nice to say about her father it reflects poorly on the daughter, huh? Don't know what it's like for my brother but everyone says the same thing to me, "Ohhhh, your father doesn't seem that bad." But he *is*, he's decisively, crushingly that bad, and nobody ever knows because, get this, he's also handsome and glamorous – sartorial splendor, what a distraction. His shoes are shiny and custom, his cuffs, French and impeccable, he smells of lime – I love lime – and when he hands you a cocktail, he hands you a small, freshly pressed napkin, too. Just in case you need a small, freshly pressed napkin. How does he have time to attend to the details, to shine all his shoes, he has a lot of shoes, I wonder, because my father's a big shot, a board-of-directors man, with a corner office, an uncluttered desk, a muffling carpet and a lady out front keeping his calendar, Violet, used to have an IBM Selectric – click, click, click – now she has a desktop Dell...whoosh. Well, not now, she's retired now, so is he, however I remember the changeover bedeviling her. But not my father, he's a speedy learner, self-made man, no old boy he, but still, nobody shines his shoes. Nobody presses his napkins either, I've watched him press his napkins, my mother simply refuses, she says, "Use paper ones with flowers, why waste the time?" My theory? The pressed napkins make him *feel* like an old boy...and that's the closest he ever comes because *real* old boys don't press napkins, do they?

    (Wait.)

And if my father wasn't a real one, my brother could never be a real one either, too bad, bet he'd have liked that.

    (Wait.)

Oh well...baffling fathers are a dime a dozen, glamorous ones are too, right? They're glamorous *because* they're baffling, isn't that one of the Ten Commandments? Or would it be the Bill of Rights, both documents definitely written for dads. And feeling baffled makes everything kind of difficult and, honestly, I pretty much feel baffled a lot now because – that's right, that's why I talked about my father – they're both baffling. See, I'm not sure Jack ever *was* listening, *just like my father*, no there is one difference, Jack makes nice faces. Wait, do we think I have daddy issues? I know, but do things become reductive and cliché because they're just true? Don't answer that, pretty much everybody has daddy issues, I should just get over it. But can you see, maybe, why – for Flo – being dumped in the middle here might be... what...disappointing? *At best* disappointing? I find it heartbreaking and disappointing, even though Flo scares me, but, know what she said? *"Mom,* **you** *are so disappointing right now, you know that, don't you?"*

    (Wait.)

No, I don't know that. But guess I know now.

    (Wait.)

By the way, Jack's an old boy. No money to speak of but you don't need money, in some ways it works great if the money's dwindled, gives an old boy a particular luster, a chance to throw his old boy DNA around in order to make the money back, or better still, prove it's not about money, it's about DNA, the magic of DNA, the force of DNA, it's DNA gets you into prep school, the Ivy League, the secret society, DNA is always Jack's barnstorming way and yes, as the most preferred leverage it's seen better days but it's not dead yet and Jack drives his like a race car, guns it, loves it, Jack is so proud of Jack.

(Wait.)

And I'm proud of Jack too, you know, how could I not be?

(Wait.)

Here's what happened. Jack was nice to me and nobody'd ever been nice to me, not like that, nobody'd ever hung on my every word, certainly not a *real* old boy, I had no reference for it, so I married him. He was also good in bed. And if you think that's a little preposterous, the truth is often a little preposterous, don't you find, I'm finding that. And could be, the reason Jack's face goes shiny when he makes me happy is he's getting a kick out of working his DNA, on me, making that magic, on me, so much magic.

(Wait.)

Imagine if I sent this to the next group that asks me to give a talk...imagine that...

(Wait.)

On my thirtieth birthday Jack gave me thirty presents, talk about a shiny face, this story is pretty important. He filled a trunk with thirty presents, we weren't

even married yet and we had no money – my father
never gave us a dime and Jack's only inheritance was
his DNA. Crazy, random stuff was in the trunk. A
cordless telephone – our crumbly apartment still had
a rotary, we thought we were the Jetsons, and if you
don't know the Jetsons it's an outer-space reference.
Tiny sapphire earrings – blink and you missed 'em,
but they *were* sapphires, nobody else in the history of
the world has ever given me jewelry. A hot blue, two-
piece outfit – tight, tight, each clingy piece counted as
a present, good eye Jack, I looked fabulous. Tickets to
the Aqueduct Racetrack in South Ozone Park, New
York – I might have given him a, you know, blow job
in the empty train car on the way home, can't be sure,
but either way, too much information. A wad of cash –
for betting, natch, I saved some to pay the light bill. A
hunk of fancy, French cheese – I thought there was only
American. A biography of Napoleon and Josephine –
what, to go with the cheese? A salad spinner – more
outer space than the phone, we used to dry the lettuce
with dish towels. Peter Gabriel's record *So* – the
album with "Sledgehammer," that song holds up, and
it wasn't a CD, it was vinyl. A *Butch Cassidy and the
Sundance Kid* t-shirt – speaks for itself. A brand-new
roll of jet-black, satin ribbon – I save all the ribbon at
Christmas but it's always wrinkled, that was the most
luxurious present. A Roller Ball pen – genius ink flow
and handwriting liberation. An Estée Lauder lipstick –
Pearl Pink, back when my everyday fav, weird he knew,
a level of observation not seen since. A lacy white
bra – fine, a present for him. Lacy white panties – fine,
another present for him. A handmade cassette of music
to shag to – Jack shagging never lets you down, count
it as an extra. A bag of fortune cookies – I may be the
only person who likes how they taste. A thirty-dollar
gift certificate to the pizza place across the street –
free food! Thirty subway tokens, remember subway
tokens? – free transportation! Thirty cans of Heineken –
free vice! A membership to the Metropolitan Museum

of Art – Jack was transferred to the DC office so we never got to use it, I was sad about that. White Ray-Ban sunglasses – I looked like Marilyn Monroe. A swanky, hotel-type bathrobe – always a sucker for swanky. The *Stop Making Sense* concert video – no words, I love the *Stop Making Sense* concert video, I love David Byrne's big suit, I understand it, Jack does not. A coffee pot – before that I always went to the deli. A tea cozy in the shape of a cat – why not? A bottle of pink champagne – first time I knew they made it in pink. A package of giant, wild cherry gumballs – still my favorite food, I deny it to the children. And a Schnauzer puppy – yup, in the trunk, somehow he was sleeping in a side compartment, we called him John the Dog, he always slept a lot. That's thirty. And since I can guess what *some people* might be thinking because these are undisputed facts and not many Jack facts are undisputed these days...I'll wait, in case anyone needs a minute to recover from the wondrous mindfuck of all this bounty, pardon my language. I'm *still* recovering and it was a long time ago.

(Wait.)

Yeah, I can guess what some people might be thinking, it's what those same people think when I talk about my father – things are connected a lot, right? It's like, "You see, people are complicated," "Don't let perfect be the enemy of good," or, everyone's favorite, "Wow." So even with *all* the things out there about Jack, *all* the things, some people are not going to budge, and since those are the people who want me to stop talking...I think I'll keep talking.

(Wait.)

I do wonder if Jack might have peaked with the trunk. I mean think about it, since he needs to make me happy a lot and also needs to keep it secret, combined with the exhaustion of the listening face situation, combined with all the plaintiffs, defendants and church steward obligations, combined with dropping everything for Eli and Flo – and did I mention, for years, he was their soccer coach, always ranked top of the league? Oh, ha, and in the early days he was a celebrity on the school's website, too...before, well it was more than ten years ago so...Jack was famous for making game-day faces on the sidelines. Making faces, duh. And they *were* funny faces, because they were extreme, but then it wasn't funny when the veins popped out of his neck after a questionable call from the lady ref, the picture on the website was very funny, but just the picture. It also wasn't funny when Jack picked up the ref's purse and, maybe, threw it at her – he certainly threw it – when they wound up alone in the faculty lounge collecting their stuff after the game. How do I know that's what happened? The ref's husband called me, said he assumed it was locker room spleen, 'bro' stuff, that he wouldn't pursue it because of the kids, but he did want to tell me. Tell me what, Jack will do anything to win? Even back then, didn't everyone know Jack will do anything to win? And why tell *me*? Why not tell *Jack*?

(Wait.)

Bro. What are you, scared of Jack?

(Wait.)

So like I say, Jack's something else too and now I bet you see it's a little slippery, right? And he might have peaked with the trunk because, in the last ten years at least, the wins have gotten harder, and the trunk had charm, now I don't see much charm, guess life wears charm away so, should I feel sorry for Jack, like maybe for my father? And sure Jack still wins, obviously he's the biggest winner, but at what cost? Also, not knowing exactly what it is Jack's trying to do because it looks like one thing but it might be another – pressed napkins, you know, or a funny face, you know – having to fill in the confusing gaps, *my* having to fill in Jack's confusing gaps is a lifetime of busy, I don't know if men do this, women definitely fucking do this – language again, sorry – it's almost like filling in the gaps *brainwashes* a person to keep filling in the gaps, the repetition brainwashes a person so that filling in the gaps – you know, disguising the fact that there *are* gaps – becomes an instinct. Hide the gaps, make the stuff that's not quite right *right*, that's the job, you're brainwashed into making sure no one clocks the stuff that's not quite right, there's so much of that stuff, so many gaps, and filling them in is on *you*, we might come back to brainwashing.

(Wait.)

She also said this...*"I'm sorry, Mom, but how come all you do is think about Dad and you* **still** *don't know anything?"*

(Wait.)

It's a fair question but I'm not sure she's correct. Some things I do know, things she doesn't, like I know what's strangely devastating – not just to me, to a lot of people – on top of everything, Jack is good-looking, and not in a showy way, he's reliably good-looking, it slinks up on you. Young, old, skinnier, fatter, Jack can be relied on to look good, bet I don't have to tell you, it's the hair. When he was younger it was bone straight, long and jet-black shiny, like the jet-black shiny birthday ribbon – ohhhhh, wait – maybe the ribbon was a thing, that never occurred to me...good detail, put it in the plus column, hardly a game changer though, right?

(Wait.)

But.

(Wait. She is visibly upset.)

Jack's hair is still long, for a middle-aged judge it's sneaky long, and he knows it, sometimes they mention it in the newspaper. Not so straight anymore, now with hair gel there's a wave. And not jet-black shiny. Salt and pepper. Better. Jet-black shiny is a dime a dozen, salt and pepper means experience and experience is so much better, how did it get better, for a long time it got better, but now, John the Dog is the longest lasting success story of my life.

(*Wait.*)

Thinking about why I'd be crazy nuts for Jack's hair upsets me every time. I feel a stab, like something savage with a razor edge penetrating my throat, so I changed the subject to John the Dog, who is *not* the longest lasting success story of my life. My children are the longest lasting success story of my life, so Flo's wrong I only think about him, *I'm thinking about my children!* And of course, Eli and Flo are harder than John the Dog because I'm custodian of their precious human souls, guardian of their fragile childhood safety, caretaker of their joyful emerging spirits and also, John was only, ever, putty in my hands, I mean when is real success easy?

(*Wait.*)

Though I do have to ask, is the prominence of an animal in any person's life objectively soulful or an adjacent shade of cat lady? Jack says that. I have to ask, also, how to keep Eli and Flo away from the 'iffy' parts of Jack, and that's hard, because they're around all the time, they were standing with me – Eli asked why Jack closed the door – in the hall outside the faculty lounge when the purse slammed into the teachers' coffee mugs and shattered them all over the linoleum. Jack said he knocked the mugs by accident but I'm almost certain they heard the ugly word he called the lady ref so, I'm not too good at keeping them away from the 'iffy' parts, am I? And Jack would never think about that but what I think about is how to hand Eli and Flo only the parts they'll like very much. Please don't forget, there are so many parts to like very much – Jack sings me love songs, Eli *still* talks about the World Series – and that's my problem, how to offer only *those* parts up on a silver platter, "Here you go, babies, from Mommy *and* Daddy, with love," I think about a strategy for doing that every day, not going to happen, is it?

(Wait.)

If you're a 'cease and desist' person, you might be worrying now.

(Wait.)

Good.

(Wait.)

So those daddy issues...I asked about things being connected, didn't I? *"Oh Mom, you're not going to try and defend yourself, are you?"* She said that. And I said, "No." But things keep popping into my head, which makes me think I know something she wants to know, let's see, because this popped into my head, so let's see, my mom told me, when I was like sixteen she told me, after my father had not done *something* – if it was regarding me my father didn't do anything, but in all fairness the same was true for my brother – wait...no...my father did take me to a Mets game once, he was shamed into it, I loved the Mets, *loved*, and I wore a special outfit to the game, I was maybe ten, I wore hot pants, all the rage in the tween set at the time, they were pretty much just shorts, but the hook to the outfit's success was calling them hot pants, sounds inappropriate, right? Which does make me wonder, and I don't want to exaggerate, but how much of my life has been inappropriate? What, maybe...an eighth?

A third? *More?* And where does that lead? What are the choices with a quantifiable amount of inappropriate?

(*Wait.*)

So there I was, wearing hot pants at Shea Stadium – my brother wasn't invited, I'm sure that made him furious, he loved the Mets too, in truth, I stole the idea of loving the Mets from my brother. It should have been heaven – didn't know it wasn't – only found out when my father had to mention that the stadium was filthy, the hot dogs made of cat meat, the smell untenable and the people, "Everything he'd devoted his life to escaping." Funny I thought he was having a good time, right? Anyway, that's my only memory of my father doing something *I* wanted to do...sooo, after he'd not done something – who knows what, it's a wasteland of empty fatherhood back there – my mother reported the following. We were walking down the stairs and she abruptly stopped, turned around, put her hand on my chest to stop me too – I almost tripped – she trapped me to make sure she had my full attention, so we were weirdly stuck in the middle of the stairs, when she said, "You know, I told your father, I thought it was entirely possible you would have trouble with men because of him." Why did she need to trap me on the stairs to tell me that when I was sixteen?

(*Wait.*)

I tried to get past my mom, to not think about what she'd said because what was I supposed to do with that piece of information, but my mom blocked me, she wanted to bring the point home, wanted it to land, and since I'm telling you about it now she must have gotten what she wanted. Yeah, I think she got it. I'm going to silently count to five before continuing.

(*Slowly mouthing the numbers.*) One. Two. Three. Four. Five.

(Talking again.) Okay. All the stories, how we got here, right? Or how I *helped* Jack get here...

   (Wait.)

I'm uncomfortable saying that.

   (Wait.)

But helping him is what I do...I've never thought about it this way before...

   (Wait.)

I wonder if Flo would laugh now.

   (Wait.)

Would Flo laugh now? At *me*?

   (Wait.)

Yup, I can keep going...so...I should take a quick sec to fill you in on Mom. And the brainwashing, remember the brainwashing – it all might be connected, or is that pretty obvious now? My mother really should be head of the World Bank, or something, the International Monetary Fund, Secretary of the Treasury, but for the brainwashing she might be, her long game with money is as good as it gets, she invested my father's and made him a mint. My father was a good earner, but money wasn't the goal, the corner office with Violet out front was the goal, the pressed napkins the ultimate goal. But without the requisite DNA, money has *got* to be the goal, so my father is kind of a weakling next to guys who spend their days hunting dollars and/or have the DNA and I bet they can just smell him. So, since my mother is the George Soros of housewives, she gave my father a big assist but, but, but the reverse trajectory of *my* dad, *her* dad, her *dad's* dad, all dads going back to the dinosaurs, the infinite bait and switch of a whole bunch of dads – *even good ones* – going down, pretty much, any rabbit hole that strikes their fancy, while my mother George Soros-es herself to death filling in dad gaps with smart short selling, brainwashed my mother, the continuous loop, brainwashed my mother to use her magnificent skills for filling in dad gaps *only*. I said, that's the job, make these guys look good, make the stuff that isn't right *right*, instead of just fucking being George Soros herself – I am not going to apologize for my language anymore! – and George could have learned stuff from my mom, who didn't have time to be George because, as I also said, filling in the gaps keeps you busy, *making sure the children don't suspect there are gaps*, *that's the big one*, and the ultimate futility of it all begs the question – after you're punched in the face with a few key facts and the brainwashing gets knocked out of you – does brainwashing start on day one? Meaning, are too many of us doomed from the beginning?

(Wait.)

"Oh come on, Mom, it's just so obvious."

(Wait. It's really not obvious.)

Jack's guacamole is fantastic. It's a party when Jack makes guacamole, Jack's really good at a party. And his friends from high school, college, law school, he stays in touch with all of them, sends handwritten cards on their birthdays, keeps an old-school wall calendar to remind him – I may be everything to Jack but he does like a crowd. A party with Jack is fun, the children say, "Dad's guac is the secret sauce." And he's particular about the chips, when Jack settles on a brand, that's it. Once he ordered twenty-four bags on the internet just to have the stock – salty and lime-flavored, Jack loves lime as much as I do. A while after, we were all in the kitchen preparing for some guests...Flo was a toddler, walking a couple of months, but she was happily playing on the floor...and Jack was making the guac when he asked if I'd noticed that the internet chips tasted different from the ones – same brand – we bought at the store, they weren't as limey, hardly salty at all, and did I think the formula had changed? I said, "*So funny*, I was wondering that exact thing when I put the bowl of chips on the coffee table, I've wondered it for a couple of months but didn't say anything." So, Jack and I deep dived about tortilla chips, we take our chips seriously, and it turned out, for a couple of months, *he'd* wondered where's the salt, where's the lime? Okay, our kitchen and living room are open-plan, no walls, and I picked up Jack's guacamole, turned to bring it to the coffee table and saw our Miss Flo in front of the chip bowl – she must have toddled over, she could do that now – and she picked up a chip, licked it on both sides, put it back in the bowl, picked up another chip, licked that one on both sides, put it back in the bowl and just kept going. No, the chip company had not changed the formula. Yes, Flo had been licking the salt and lime off the chips since she learned to walk...and we'd fed bowls and bowls of those chips to our guests! Jack started to get mad but Flo gave him a sly boots look, making it clear she knew she was a naughty girl, while at the same time *daring* Jack to get mad, *"Go on Daddy, give it your best shot, I bet you can't resist me but...try."* She was right, Jack couldn't resist her, he laughed his socks off, let her lick as many chips as she wanted and put her to bed with love when she got the tummy ache. Lucky we had all those back-up chips in the pantry.

(Wait. Her amusement slowly fades.)

But know what I'm thinking about that sly boots look now? I'm thinking, at fifteen months old, Flo was filling in a gap.

(Wait.)

So having a go at the Catholic Church is tired and there are a billion good deeds performed under their banner,

but the whole institution is one of the more spectacular
gap-filling entities – yes, everything *is* connected. I
won't spend time on the church's problematic power
structure *or* its fake explanations for nature's mysteries
but there was a weird thing that happened. I was
probably nine, and for years I couldn't sleep, 'til I
was eleven or more, because I felt guilty, so I went to
confession thinking if I was forgiven then maybe I
could sleep. The essential thing here is that confession
is anonymous except, to this day, I do not know if mine
was because when the priest pulled back the little door
in the confessional it was Father Patel, who had just
been to our house for Easter and, even though a screen
is supposed to keep everyone in the dark, I knew it was
Father Patel because of his accent. He was on a one-
year posting from his regular parish in India and since
I'd just spent four hours with him around our dining
room table – every year my mother gives guests hand-
painted Easter eggs, he went NUTS for his, it had
crucifixes on it – I worried he knew it was me. But I'd
walked all the way alone, it was like three miles, six with
the walk back – I didn't want my mother to know – so
I confessed to Father Patel and he said, "Did anything
happen?" That's it, that's all he said, "Did anything
happen?" When I said, "No," because somehow I knew
what he meant, he seemed relieved so we moved on –
the next thing I confessed was stealing Twizzlers from
my brother's Easter basket. And I should tell you, what
Father Patel meant was, did a baby happen, and my
answer was no, which was true, except something *did*
happen. My brother, who was older, *did* try to have
sex with me, a few times, I'm not strictly sure if he
succeeded, but he asked me if it was "in" and I said I
didn't know, that part's pretty memorable. However,
Father Patel didn't seem interested in that part, or any
of the other parts, he just told me to say two Hail Marys
and one Our Father and I'd be good to go. That's all. I
guess he forgave me, but I still couldn't sleep, I think

because I was always feeling like I shouldn't have let my brother do it, I definitely was guilty there, and even worse, now I had to worry Father Patel knew it was me whenever I saw him, which I did every day until school was over in late June, so it all took up a lot of my time when I was nine, ten, eleven, for a while, Eli and Flo don't know any of this.

(*Wait.*)

Lots of things that have happened since could have been filling in that brother gap, right? Or maybe that was filling in another gap? My mother'd say *everything's* about filling in the dad gap if she knew, which she doesn't – well she knew my brother tried something like that when I was seven or eight but she just said I could maybe get pregnant so we had better stop...wait, we?...wow.

(*Wait.*)

I'm pretty sure putting Jack, my mom, George Soros, my father, Father Patel, my brother, Eli and Flo, all in the same giant thought bubble would never have occurred to me if Mom hadn't said what she said on the stairs – oh, and this just came into my mind, I *am* the giant thought bubble. Also, the deeper Jack and I get into it, my mother saying, "I told your father, I thought it was entirely possible you would have trouble with men because of him," sounds louder in my ear. But now that I have to get out of it – since the water main break in my daughter's brain created such a mess I have to get out of it – getting out requires me to get more deeply in. And how do I get out? I'm brainwashed too, not sure what to do, and that was never true, I was a can-do gal, but the listening face, and the hot pants, the *Stop Making Sense* video, the one-time-only Mets game, salt and pepper hair, brother, pressed napkins, why did Mom say that, are Eli and Flo ruffled by their father's face, everything makes me think

it's true a whole lot of us *are* doomed from the start,
and that's by stuff that won't technically kill us – not
guns, cancer, nukes, famine – that's by mostly cushy
stuff, stuff pretty much everyone wants, who *doesn't*
want the *Stop Making Sense* video? But doom, to me,
feels it should definitely be about no food, no shelter
or murder. I've always had food, shelter and never any
murder but still, no compass, and a slim skill set to find
north, recognize what's solidly true, I don't even know
what a solidly true *face* looks like, is that because of the
brainwashing? Or because the people who should have
taught me don't know either? Or...or if they do know
they're not telling? I guess so they can do what's good
for them? Okay...being afraid the people charged with
having my interests at heart are selfish and I never
knew it – mighta been the case my whole life and I
missed it – but then it just got said, ten years ago she
said it, in front of all the senators she said it, lucidly,
unambiguously, with guts, she said what happened to
her, on TV for the whole nation to witness, she said Jack
did that to her when she was just in high school and he
was in high school too, and ninety percent of everyone
listening maybe knew Jack *did* do it, those senators
maybe knew, but they voted for him anyway, do you
figure that's because a lot of them did something like
that, too? I mean a lot of men do that and the senators
on the committee were all men, at the time, all of them,
like I said, everything is connected.

    (Wait.)

And I wonder, did my brother think about what he did
to me when he watched her on TV? Then again, did he
even watch since he knew what she was going to say? I
bet a lot of men didn't even watch.

    (Wait.)

I'm in the ten percent that maybe doesn't know if Jack did it

doesn't want to know if Jack did it

can't know if Jack did it

oh, if Eli and Flo could never know

I hunted and hunted for a way Eli and Flo could never know

I kept them from knowing for such a long time,

my finest achievement, it was the one,

I filled in that gap and they were grateful,

so grateful I only confirmed the best of their dad

and they believed me, believed me so hard,

then Flo grew up and didn't, she didn't believe me anymore

had her own beautiful mind and didn't believe me anymore

went to her fancy college, did her homework, and didn't believe me

anymore

so I didn't believe me

anymore

it happened when Flo came home for the summer

after she took Constitutional Law

after the section on politics in the modern Supreme Court

which was after Flo kept her father's job a secret

told every new friend he was just a lawyer

which was after she got to her liberal, liberal arts college

which was after she scrubbed her Facebook page, took weeks to erase our family

after all that Flo asked me, *"Do you ever feel bad that you just sat there letting that woman twist in the wind?"*

(Wait.)

When I was able to speak, I said, "What?"

"Mom, you heard me."

(Wait.)

"Flo, I have nothing to do with that woman."

"That's not true, is it Mom?"

(Wait.)

And then I said a thing I'd never said before. And then I said, "Every day. I feel bad every day. I think of that woman, ten years, every day."

"Good. She was brave. And you know it."

"Yes."

"The senators dripped sugar from their mouths but treated her like crummy garbage all the same."

"Yes."

"Did you tell Dad you thought she was brave?"

"No."

"Why not, Mom?"

"We don't talk about her."

"Back then, did you tell Dad you thought she was brave back then!"

"I was busy telling Dad *he* was brave, busy filling in the gaps, I sat behind him, filled in the most looming gap, nobody knew there was a gap, I did that, they wouldn't have voted for him if I didn't do that."

"But he hurt her, Mom. In high school, he hurt her, it's the same old story, a million guys taking what they want, a million girls scared forever, that's what they get.

And Dad's a worthless piece of shit for lying about it, for getting the job – that job, the country could be at his mercy for forty years! – only by lying about it. He's my father, I love him, I have to figure it out, but that's what I think."

"Flo, he didn't lie, he can't remember ever hurting her."

"He was drunk, it doesn't matter he can't remember, it's his privilege not to remember, those senators hoped he wouldn't remember, but he so obviously did it, Mom."

"How is it obvious, Flo?"

"Are you serious?! Jesus Christ, Mom, did you even listen to her?!"

　(Wait.)

"No."

"No? You didn't listen to her? How is that possible?"

"I saw the twisted and terrified look on her face and tried my hardest not to listen, Flo."

"That's not a thing, that can't be done, a person can't do that!"

"I CAN DO IT, I LEARNED FROM THE PROS!"

"What the fuck, Mom?!"

"I'm sorry, Flo! I'm very sorry!"

"I DO NOT FORGIVE YOU, I NEVER WILL, YOU SHOULD BE ASHAMED OF YOURSELF!"

　(Wait.)

"And so I am, Flo. For years and years, long before *her*, but she sure helps, that one's in the bag, it's all yours, sweetheart."

　(Wait.)

I didn't mean to sound aggressive, like I said, I don't blame Flo – oh no, no, no – I admire her, couldn't do it myself and it scares me to watch, but you go, Flo, take no prisoners.

   (Wait.)

If Jack is selfish, his listening no more listening than my father's – an irony since a Supreme Court justice's job is to listen – if Jack's listening is really taking, if making me happy means I'll sit behind him, since if I do he must be making me happy so he must be a great guy, not the guy *she* says but a great guy, how's a regular person, like me, *supposed to know how not to just sit there?!* Because I'm regular but nothing that happened is regular. Except, will Eli and Flo think it *is* regular? Only oops, Jack got caught. But wait, Jack got away with it, is it regular they think their father gets away with being selfish and dangerous? And do they think *I'm* selfish and dangerous? Am I?

   (Wait.)

My brother got away with it too, guess it all *is* pretty regular. And if I *am* selfish and dangerous, well, that's pretty regular, also. I'm regular stuffing. I fill in a gap, Jack *is* the gap and he's a tight squeeze. It's also regular the senators voted for him...the devil you know. And regular, too, they drip sugar on that woman's head until she suffocates and dies.

   (Wait.)

And another thing about DNA...Eli worships his dad, Jack likes it that way, they speak in code, feeding one another 'bro' stuff. But in Jack's world where *I* am everything – or at least that's his exhausting story – he doesn't need his children to be everything too, under the circumstances they're not quite as useful. So in a world where Eli thinks *he's* everything...but he's not... I need to take care of Eli because what does he really know? Okay, he knows he wants to go to law school, be a judge, like Jack, he even says, "I've got the DNA, don't I, Dad?" But what else does Eli know? For so many reasons, not good if he knows the rest, is it? And if he does know, not good he worships his dad, is it? And would *he* ever...? But maybe Eli doesn't know. In a hopeful moment, I asked Flo not to talk to her brother about Constitutional Law, he's three years younger, just sixteen, doesn't seem he needs to explode – I'm sure Flo wants him to – but also, willful ignorance runs in our family and I'm all for Eli's willful ignorance, not proud of that but having failed with Flo might kill me, you see I believe her, Flo will never forgive me. And it's not a teenage tantrum, look in her eyes, she can't love me anymore.

(Wait.)

Guess I got mine.

(Wait.)

Please remember the most important thing. Jack was kind. His face always composed, looking like it was his privilege to listen. Why is that the most important thing? Because that is the information I had, for a long time that is what I knew and it was so overpowering that was *everything* I knew. But maybe my mother was right, because the face *looked* pretty different, but it *felt* pretty familiar. Flo says, *"Really Mom, you couldn't figure **that** out, I think it's on Page One of the handbook."* Yes, shame on me.

(Wait.)

I don't know...maybe that's how I could just sit there? Or maybe, I *wanted* what Jack said to be true so I sat there to *make* it true. Then Flo came home and it couldn't be true, said she'd never forgive me so it couldn't be true, but please don't tell Eli, please don't, not yet.

(Wait.)

Even if you don't, or even if you do, what's really left? Nothing's really left. I thought making this might...

(Wait.)

No.

(Wait.)

Okay, I'll tell you another secret...this one's only mine... all the stories are really about me. Thought I'd hook you with Jack stuff, knew that's why you'd care, because who wants stories about me, I mean really. And you 'cease and desist' people, you don't have to worry a single lick, do you? The Jack stuff everyone knows... *everyone* knows about Jack...now Jack does, too.

(Wait.)

And life goes on, doesn't it? Doesn't it always?

(Wait.)

By the way, my name is Mary. No one remembers, but my name is Mary. Hello.

(Blackout.)

End of Play

www.ingramcontent.com/pod-product-compliance
Lightning Source LLC
Chambersburg PA
CBHW070403120726
47909CB00008B/2977